16

Is great **teamwork** important to you? Read about *Jubilee*

18

Are you **bold** and **adventurous?** Turn to *America Chavez*

20

Would you like to **teach others?** Meet *Professor X*

22

Do you love **truth** and **justice?** See brave *Captain America*

24

Do you have **big dreams?** Be like *Moon Girl*

26

Want to **focus** your skills to overcome **challenges?** See *Hawkeye*

28

Are you **cool** but **kind-hearted?** Learn about *Ironheart*

30

Are you interested in **magic** and **mystery?** Find out about *Doctor Strange*

Ms Marvel

I was just an ordinary 16-year-old schoolgirl. Then one day, I walked through a strange mist. It changed me and gave me new powers. I became stretchy like elastic!

Now I can take any shape I like. I can be tall or small, whatever I choose! I am fast and flexible, too. I took on the Super Hero name Ms Marvel to honour my favourite hero, Captain Marvel. Now I'm doing things my own way!

I am...

A smart student

A kind and funny friend

Using my powers for good

My hobbies

Playing video games

Computer programming with Squirrel Girl

Writing my own Super Hero stories

Black Panther

My name is T'Challa and I am king of Wakanda.
I trained for this role from a young age.
Some people want to destroy my nation,
so I must protect it and my people.

I am also the warrior known as
the Black Panther. I am strong,
stealthy, and fast. Like a real
panther, I use all my senses
to hunt down my foes.
Then I pounce!

I am...

A fair leader

A kind brother to
my sister, Shuri

Proud of my country

My hobbies

Martial arts

Trying out Shuri's new
weapons and gadgets

Learning languages from
around the world

My hobbies

Organising computer-science classes

Climbing trees

Babysitting for other Super Heroes

Squirrel Girl

I am Doreen Green and I am extraordinary! I was born with a squirrel's teeth, tail, and ears. I can bite through wood and swing from my bushy tail. If anyone teases me, I ignore them. I know my squirrel-like skills are special and I use them to fight crime.

I can talk to squirrels, too. My Best Squirrel Friend Forever (BSFF) is Tippy Toe. She likes to drink acorn smoothies. Yum!

I am...

Fast-talking and funny

Always looking for the good in people, even villains

Not afraid of anyone

My hobbies

Studying my favourite school subjects

Swinging through the city

Hanging out with my best friend, Ganke

Spider-Man

Did you know that there are many heroes called Spider-Man? I am Miles Morales and I am one of them. I come from another version of Earth, but I moved worlds. When I was 13, a special spider bit me. It gave me spider-powers!

I can climb up buildings with my sticky hands and feet and run after villains really fast. When I catch them, I fire webs from my wrists to trap them. I can sense when danger is coming, too.

I am...

A great team player

Quick to help people in trouble

Adapting to life in this version of New York City

Captain Marvel

I joined the US Air Force when I was 18. My nickname was Cheeseburger! I was the fastest pilot, but some people thought I was not good enough because I was a girl. So I joined NASA, where I flew to space.

When I discovered I had alien powers, I learnt to fly without needing a spaceship! I can also lift incredibly heavy objects and blast energy bolts from my hands.

My hobbies

Saving planets from alien invasions

Playing with my alien cat

Writing magazine articles

I am...

Half-alien Kree and half human

Fluent in many languages

A strong leader

Brawn

I am the eighth smartest guy on Earth. I once won a competition to prove it! Some people think being as brainy as me is dangerous, so I have many enemies. Luckily, Bruce Banner, also known as the Hulk, looks out for me. I share his powers, so now I am big, green, and strong as well as smart!

My brain works very fast, like a computer. This uses up a lot of energy, so I am often hungry!

My hobbies

Computer hacking

Solving maths problems

Helping my teammates, the Champions

I am...

Always green

A genius

Called Amadeus Cho for the composer Wolfgang Amadeus Mozart

Jubilee

My super-powers took me by surprise. One day when I was running away from trouble, I realised I could produce fireworks and blasts of energy from my hands!

I joined the Super Hero group called the X-Men. I help bring criminals to justice. I try to do it without hurting anyone. Even criminals!

My hobbies

Skateboarding and rollerblading

Gymnastics

Computer games

I am...

Learning to be a leader

Strong-willed and determined

Not good at maths but good at being a hero!

17

America Chavez

I am one of a kind! I can smash star-shaped portals through entire galaxies and then travel through them. Since my own world was destroyed, I have made it my job to protect other planets, including Earth.

I can fly through space at super speeds. I have even been to a university on another world! I am super strong, too. One stamp of my feet can defeat any foe.

My hobbies

Learning how to travel through time

Improving my fighting skills

Making new friends on different planets

I am...

Travelling through many galaxies

Fluent in both Spanish and English

Always ready for action!

18

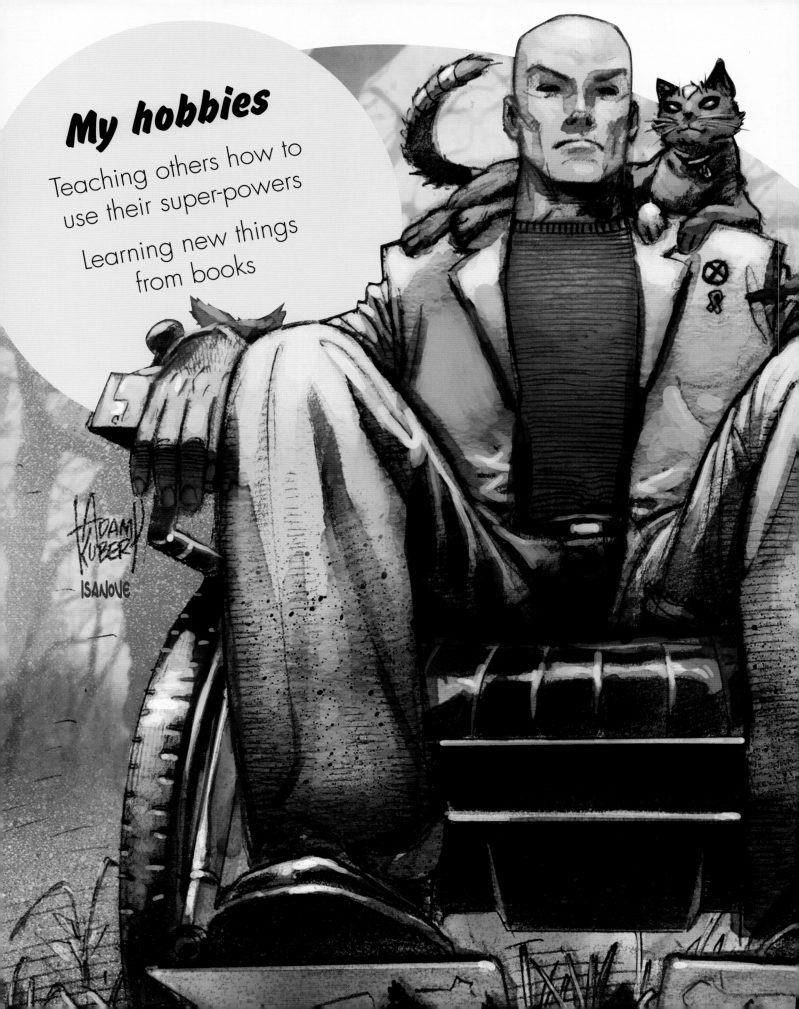

My hobbies

Teaching others how to use their super-powers

Learning new things from books

Professor X

I was born with the ability to read people's thoughts and feelings! I can move objects with my mind, too. I run a special school where others born with powers can develop their skills. Many ordinary people do not trust us. I hope to change that and bring peace.

After a fight with some enemies, I now use a wheelchair, but I am still battling evil. I also started the famous Super Hero team called the X-Men.

I am...

Highly intelligent

A professor specialising in science

One of the most powerful heroes on Earth!

Captain America

Once, I was so weak and small that the army would not let me join. But then I agreed to test a special serum. It made me super strong and fast! I was not just Steve Rogers any more, I was mighty Captain America!

I protect anyone in need using my unbreakable shield. I heal quickly from injuries, and I stay calm at all times. Being calm helps me in battle!

My hobbies

Finding more heroes to join the Avengers team

Practising throwing and catching my shield

Martial arts and acrobatics

I am...

Loyal to my friends

A kind and caring leader

Determined to fight for what is right

Moon Girl

I am only nine years old, but I am already a hero! I fight crime with my best friend, Devil Dinosaur. He is a T. rex who came striding through a portal from another land!

Science is my favourite subject. I love building gadgets and have made a jetpack and roller skates to help me zoom around faster. My school friends call me a daydreamer, but I know that my ideas could change the world.

I am...

A science genius

Part of a special human race called the Inhumans

Not scared of things bigger than me

My hobbies

Reading books

Inventing technology in my secret lab

Using mind power to talk to my T. rex

Hawkeye

I have no super-powers, but that does not stop me from being a hero. All I need is my bow, a quiver full of arrows, and my eagle-eye vision. I am Hawkeye, and I am the best archer around!

Being deaf does not hold me back. Iron Man has made me high-tech hearing aids, and I use sign language.

I am...

A loyal Avenger

Eagle-eyed like a real hawk

Skilled at hand-to-hand combat

My hobbies

Acrobatics and circus tricks

Spending time with my favourite dog, Lucky

Ironheart

I was just 15 when I started university. They let me start early because of my talent for engineering. It was there that I made my first suit of flying armour. When Iron Man saw it, he was so impressed he offered to help me become a Super Hero!

I have lost dear friends and family members. My Super Hero name is my way of keeping their memory close.

My hobbies

Engineering and inventing new gadgets

Computer coding

Playing video games

I am...

Quick to solve problems

Learning not to rush in to situations

Kind-hearted

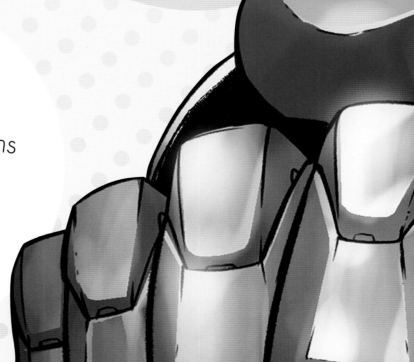

28

Doctor Strange

I wasn't always a Super Hero. I used to be the best surgeon in the world, until I was injured in a serious car accident. After this, I could no longer use my hands for my job, so I trained to use magic instead.

Now I can cast spells and read minds. A special cloak helps me to fly. I can also travel wherever I like, by thinking about where I want to go.

My hobbies

Meditating

Exploring other worlds and travelling through time

I am...

Mysterious and powerful

Learning to help others as well as myself

A supremely skilled sorcerer

Senior Editor Emma Grange
Project Art Editor Jessica Tapolcai
Editor Julia March
Pre-Production Producer Siu Yin Chan
Senior Producer Mary Slater
Managing Editor Sarah Harland
Managing Art Editor Vicky Short
Publisher Julie Ferris
Art Director Lisa Lanzarini

First published in Great Britain in 2020
by Dorling Kindersley Limited
80 Strand, London, WC2R 0RL
A Penguin Random House Company

10 9 8 7 6 5 4 3 2 1
001–316351–Feb/2020

©2020 MARVEL

A CIP catalogue record for this book
is available from the British Library.
ISBN 978-0-24140-891-9

Printed and bound in China

A WORLD OF IDEAS:
SEE ALL THERE IS TO KNOW

www.dk.com